STEALING THEIR FOREVER

LONNIE DORIS

THANK YOU TO TERRI ANNE...

Special thanks to Terri Anne Browning for lending me the use of some of your words to bring this novella to life. You are such an inspiration in all that I do in my life. I fell in love with your books from *The Rocker Who Holds Me* and have waited with bated breath for each one to keep me in the universe of Demon's Wings and OtherWorld, but most of all, the stories of Emmie and Drake. You never disappoint. Thank you for taking me on this journey with you. I'm so excited for everything we have planned for the future. I am so honored to work with you, but more importantly, to call you one of my closest friends.

Loves and Kisses and all that Rocks in between.

XOXO

~LD

DEAR READERS

This is Helena's story. I felt like I wanted to see what drove her to the levels of crazy Terri Anne Browning described to us in her The Rockers...Series. There are parts of this novella that incorporate Terri Anne's words. There are some scenes in this novella that are taken directly (word for word, with Terri Anne's permission) from The Rocker Who Shatters Me, The Rocker Who Hates Me, *and* Forever Rockers.

In fact, a whole lineup of The Rockers...Series Characters You Hate *is in the works.*

Next Up: Tommy Kirkman.

A NOTE FROM TERRI ANNE BROWNING

Before you start, please know that Lonnie Doris has my full permission to write Stealing Their Forever. *We consulted throughout the production of this book, so anything you are about to read has already been 100% approved by me.*

Lonnie is very dear to me, and I was the one to suggest she write this book featuring Helena. I was curious about her, but I couldn't get into her head as deeply as I needed to in order to give her story the depth it deserves. I think Lonnie did a kick-ass job with Helena's crazy and putting true emotion into her.

With the start of this book, I—and Lonnie—hope to bring you other exciting things in the future.

As always, thank you for making this such a success and supporting The Rocker...Series Universe. *None of this would be possible without you.*

All my love,

TAB

PROLOGUE

"Daddy, please," I beg. "Please just let me follow the tour for the remaining Demon's Wings concerts."

My mother and father want me to jump right into a journalism career. I just graduated from college; I think I deserve a break. But really, I have no desire to work a day in my life. If I can just hold them off a little longer, I will find myself a rich husband to ensure I can live that dream. Truth be told, if I have my way, that husband will be the bassist for my favorite rock band, Demon's Wings.

"Young lady, I have had about enough of your whining for one afternoon. Your father and I—" my mother starts before I cut her off.

"Mother, all I am asking for is six concerts, full VIP treatment, backstage and all, then I will come home and settle into my journalism career." I explain to her with a roll of my eyes. It sounds like I am asking for a lot, but it truly isn't. It isn't like they can't afford it.

"Helena, you have had your fun the whole time you were in college. It's time to take life seriously," my father scolds, but it's halfhearted to my ears.

"Daddy, if you let me do this, I will use my journalism skills and write about the experience. Let's call it an unofficial internship," I say, batting my eyelashes at him. He tries to be as hard as Mother when she is in the room, but when it is just him and me, I have him wrapped around my little finger. Daddy doesn't like to tell me no. He only does it to please Mother.

"I will discuss this with your mother," my father responds with a clenched jaw, while Mother huffs from across the table.

I turn and leave the sitting room and head upstairs to my room, slamming my door. I fall back onto my bed. I'm not defeated yet. But everything is a fight with them. Mostly, with my mother—she's the bad cop, never wants me to have any fun. Her idea of fun is her little cocktail parties so Daddy can schmooze all the rich investors for his software company.

I'm a trust-fund brat, and I like it that way. I didn't even want to go to college, but Mother won that battle. I showed her, though; I picked journalism as my major. It seemed like the easiest choice at the time. I figured it wouldn't be so bad if I ended up in front of a camera reporting the news. That's a last resort, however. I will land myself a rich husband, and I won't have to work.

As I lie on my bed, plotting my next move if they say no, there is a knock at my door.

"Come in."

I look over as the door opens, and I see my father walking into my room. I sit up in my bed, swinging my legs off the side, and look at him.

"Helena, we are going to allow you to have what you have requested," he starts, and I jump off the bed and make my way over to him to hug his neck. He has just made me the happiest girl on the planet. But he stops me before I reach him by putting his hands up. He continues, "There are conditions here, Helena, and you need to understand them. We are serious this time."

"Yes, Daddy. I know. I suggested the conditions," I respond.

"Then it should make it easier for you to live up to your deal, young lady. Your mother and I have accepted the terms you have presented. You will write about your experience traveling, watching this band, and we will provide all your expenses. Upon your return, you will begin your career as a journalist."

"Thank you, Daddy," I say as I finally get to hug him.

"You have great potential, Helena. Don't let it slip away," he says before walking out the door and leaving me alone in my room.

I pick up my phone and call my cousin Sean.

"Guess who's going to see the last six concerts of Demon's Wings?" I brag with a giddy laugh. "That's right—me. See you in a little bit." I press end on my phone and place it back on my nightstand.

While waiting for Sean to come over, I begin looking through my gigantic walk-in closet for outfits to take with me for my legendary journey.

I pull out my suitcases to get myself organized. While going through my makeup case, I find my bottle of pills. When I was in junior high school, I was diagnosed with bipolar. I'm sure it was just my mother's way of getting me to stop being high-strung—at least, *she* always thought I was. As long as she had me medicated, she thought she could control me more easily.

I'm not taking these pills with me. I want to have fun, not feel like I'm in a fog. That's how these pills affect me. I hide them in one of my drawers and continue with my packing.

The last thing I want Shane to know is that I'm supposed to take these pills to control my disorder. Just because my mother wants to believe I have bipolar doesn't mean I have to. I know once I am on the road and in front of Shane—and he falls in love with me—I won't have mood swings anymore. I won't have a reason to. My mother causes my moods, mostly the depression and sadness. She can't see it, so I have given up trying to make her.

With each item of clothing I pack, the more the excitement takes me over. I cannot wait to get on the road. The road that leads to my forever with Shane.

ONE

The backstage VIP area has everything from gourmet hors d'oeuvres to fancy desserts and every type of alcohol anyone could possibly want. Emmie Jameson sure does go all out for the fans. But then again, the fans who are back in this area have paid a pretty price to be here. I have a lot of competition around me. Females of all shapes, boob sizes, and hair color are everywhere.

The guys of Demon's Wings hang out in this area before and after their concert. This is where they pick the girls who will stay with them for the night. It's no secret Shane Stevenson is who I have my eye on, and only he will do.

I'm lost in my thoughts, looking through the crowd to see if I can spot Shane, and then I turn and run right into him.

My heart immediately begins racing. Here he is; I'm face-to-face with Shane Stevenson. His hair is a mess, but it's so sexy around his gorgeous face. His jeans fit him just right, and that sexy-ass Demon's Wings T-shirt is stretched across his chest. The sight of him is making my mouth water, but I can't manage to find my words.

"Sorry, darlin'," he says in his raspy voice.

But before I can respond, he moves past me to grab the hands of two average-looking females. Neither one of them looks like they know how to contour their faces, let alone how to suck his dick. Feeling deflated, I walk over to the bar and order a shot of tequila before I head to the pit area for the concert.

Shane momentarily rejecting me is not going to deter me. I want Shane Stevenson. I know if I can get him in bed, he will fall in love with me and we can start our life together. I will have the best of both worlds—my parents off my back and the hottest man in America as my husband. Every woman with a working vagina wants Shane, and he will be all mine. All those chicks will hate me, but I don't give a fuck.

The tabloids have it wrong; he isn't the hell-raising dick they portray him to be. Shane is just looking for love. Once he is with me, he will find it. I know he's waiting for me to come along. I will change his world.

I make my way to the pit area because Demon's Wings is about to take the stage. The music is great, but I don't expect anything less from this band. They put on a great show. I'm rocking out when I lose my footing and bump into a solid chest. Strong arms wrap around me to prevent me from falling. When I lift my head to see who my savior is, I find a handsome man with dark eyes and bronzed skin.

"I've got you, sweetheart," he says

"Thank you." His dark eyes look deep into mine. But this guy doesn't look like he belongs at a Demon's Wings concert, much less in the pit. He looks more refined than the rest of the guys banging their heads. I can see the heat burning in his eyes, and I know he is definitely attracted to me.

"I'm Reginald," he says.

"Helena." I cock my head in curiosity. "Can I ask you something?"

"Sure," he responds with a grin.

"What brings you to a Demon's Wings concert? You don't fit the rock band type."

"I'm the editor at *Rock America*. I'm covering the concert for a story about the band," he says with a shrug.

Editor and not of just any magazine, but *Rock America*, the most popular and reputable magazine in the country. The wheels in my brain immediately start turning. This guy is going to come in handy for me if I don't land Shane. I decide right then to turn my charm up a notch. I may not be sharing a bed with Shane tonight, but that doesn't mean I can't share it with Reginald. He's good-looking enough, and from the way he is looking at me, I know he wants me.

"I just graduated college with a journalism degree. I'd love to pick your brain on how to get my foot in the door somewhere. Let's blow this place and go somewhere quieter," I suggest in a sultry purr.

"I really want to, but I'm supposed to—"

I place my finger over his lips to stop him from talking anymore.

"Please," I say, looking up at him through my lashes.

Reginald looks from me to the band onstage, then back to me.

"I can catch up with them at their next stop." He places his hand at the small of my back as we walk out of the venue toward the valet attendant.

He helps me into a black Jaguar. It's a sweet ride and screams money. We drive back to his hotel, making small talk along the way. Once we arrive, we make our way to his suite. Reginald orders us a bottle of wine from room service.

We sit on the sofa and talk about the classes we both took in college while we wait for the wine to arrive. When there's a knock on the door, he gets up and returns with the wine and two glasses. We sit and sip the delicious red, and he asks about my career plans now that I've graduated.

I'm getting bored with the conversation because, even with my degree, I will never work for him—or anyone else, for that matter. I reach over and take his glass out of his hand.

"Let's take this conversation into the bedroom," I suggest.

"Isn't that supposed to be my line?" he asks, lifting a brow.

"I go after what I want. No sense playing coy, is there? I want you between my thighs." I stand up and begin to strip off my clothes on my way into the bedroom, dropping my shirt as I walk. When I get to the door, I turn around to see him behind me. He grabs me up in his arms, kissing me passionately, and carries me to the large king in the bedroom.

After he places me on my feet at the side of the bed, I unbutton his shirt and push it off his shoulders. He starts kissing my shoulder, working his way up my neck. When he reaches my mouth, his tongue dives in. He is definitely a good kisser. It makes it easier for me to replace his face with Shane's. I should be in Shane's arms right now, but I can fantasize it's really him and not Reginald kissing me like this.

He moans into my mouth, and I can feel his arousal pushing against me through his pants. His hands are roaming all over my body, sending tingles from the tips of my toes to the top of my head. Reginald pushes me back onto the bed and quickly removes my jeans and panties. He stares down at me, eyes filled with desire.

I bite down on my bottom lip, He has me more aroused than I should be, and if he doesn't touch me soon, I will take matters into my own hands.

The next morning, I wake to an empty bed and the sound of the shower running. Reginald definitely knows how to satisfy a woman in need. I slowly get out of bed and head to the bathroom to join him when I glance at the dresser and see his press pass.

Without second-guessing myself, I grab it and place it in my purse.

That little badge may just come in handy.

TWO

It's the night of my final Demon's Wings concert. This is my last chance to get Shane in bed so he can realize he's in love with me, and then we can get married and I can be with him on every tour. I've amped up the sexiness with the outfit I've picked. If this doesn't turn Shane's head, then I'm stuck with Reginald. The reality is, he's been spoiling me with nice gifts and fancy outings during the few days we've spent together in between concerts. I mean, I could do worse, but Shane is who I want more than anything.

I show my stolen press credentials as I walk into the back entrance of the arena.

I've got one goal and one goal only. This is it. I make my way through the crowd that has already assembled backstage before the show. Some of the faces are familiar, but the majority of them I have never seen before. I mingle, but I have not even seen a glimpse of Shane. I continue to walk around backstage, looking in different rooms, but I still have no luck in finding the Demon.

Feeling confident he isn't coming to the backstage area tonight, I make my way to the pit. The lights dim, indicating the band is about to take the stage. The arena erupts in screams and cheers as the fog starts filling the stage.

Shane takes his spot, and I don't take my eyes off him all night. I *have* to get him to see me. I know once his eyes meet mine, he will see my desire for him and realize I'm the one for him. We were made for each other. He just needs to see it.

And then it happens.

Shane looks down at me and winks. I blow him a kiss back. Shane's eyes make contact with mine frequently over the course of the set, like he can't stop himself. Like he needs to constantly have his eyes on me to remind himself I'm real. At one point, he motions his head, indicating for me to meet him backstage.

As Nik sings the first line of the closing song, I make my way toward the backstage area, indicating to Shane with a nod of my head that I will meet him. He grins wickedly down at me, causing my belly to flip.

I knew tonight would be the night he noticed me.

As I stand backstage waiting for Shane, other girls and security start filling the area to wait on the band. I quickly switch out my press badge for my VIP badge. I don't want to have to explain to Shane why or how I actually came by the press credential, and I don't want to have to come up with a clever lie. That's no way to start a relationship. I want a lasting romantic partnership with him. Shane is my forever.

I spot him immediately, and our gazes lock, making my heart start to pound in anticipation. He makes his way through the crowd backstage to where I am leaning against a wall.

"Hey there, pretty girl. What's your name?"

"Helena."

"I was hoping you would be back here waiting for me," he says, leaning down to kiss my neck.

"Well, here I am. What do you want to do with me?" I ask, running my hands down his chest.

"I can think of a few things," he whispers into my ear, making me shiver.

"I can think of a few things I want to do to you too." I murmur back. "But I don't share well. I want you all to myself."

"Do you think you can handle me all by yourself?"

"I know I can."

"Well, let's get out of here, then... But, pretty girl—" he pins me with his eyes "—if I become too much to handle, we will call in reinforcements." Then, taking my hand, he leads me out the back of the arena to a waiting SUV.

He helps me into the back seat, climbs in behind me, and directs the driver to the hotel where he's staying.

THREE

Glancing at the clock, I see it's just after nine in the morning. Checkout isn't until twelve. Breathing a sigh of relief, I drop back down on the pillows. Shane is probably helping the roadies load the buses and the huge semi that hauls all the band's equipment and stage gear. He'll be back for his case—and me—any minute now.

I lie there for a while longer, happier than I've ever been in my life. This is it. I've found the man I want to spend my happily ever after with. I know my parents are going to be upset that it is with a rocker rather than the Ivy League asshole they thought I should settle down with, but that just isn't me. If they don't like me marrying Shane Stevenson, they can go fuck themselves. And it isn't like I would be throwing their money in their faces without a dime to fall back on. Shane is a successful rock star. With his adopted sister's help, the band is reputed to be one of the most financially stable in the industry. He has enough money to keep me happy for the rest of our lives.

Grinning to myself at that thought, I tuck the covers

under my arms a little better and reach for the remote to the television on the nightstand. Before my fingertips can brush it, there is the distinct sound of a keycard sliding into the door. I lift my head, offering Shane a bright smile as the door opens.

A harassed-looking Emmie Jameson walks in with two roadies behind her. If Emmie weren't supposedly Shane's adopted sister, I would be jealous of the girl. With her long auburn hair, big green eyes set in a beautiful face, and a tiny body like I've spent most of my life practically starving myself to achieve, she is definitely rival material. But since she's Shane's family, that means she is going to be my family, so I offer her a dimmer version of the smile I had ready for Shane just moments before.

"Hi," I greet her as I sit up in bed. I keep the covers tucked around me so as not to flash the two roadies who are already picking up Shane's huge case and checking the room over to make sure nothing else is forgotten.

Emmie barely spares me a second glance as she moves around the room like a whirlwind. "You're still here?" She sighs and rolls her green eyes. "Awesome. He's always leaving me to take out the trash."

The bite to her tone along with her bitchy words have my spine stiffening. "Excuse me?" Who does this bitch think she is talking to? I don't care if she is family or not, I am not going to let this little slut talk to me like that. I am better than her in every way. Just because she is Shane's precious little Emmie doesn't mean shit to me. I'll make sure real fast that Precious Emmie doesn't stick around for long.

She isn't even paying attention to me, though. "Pock, take the case down and put it on the bus. Make sure Shane knows I'm not happy."

The roadie named Pock chuckles. "Sure thing, Emmie." Shooting me an amused grin, Pock lifts the heavy case and heads out the door.

The second roadie stands by the still-open door, looking menacing as he glances from me to Emmie and back again. I glare at him, daring him to say a word.

Something lands beside me on the bed, and my eyes go straight to whatever it is Emmie has just thrown at me. A wad of cash. At least three hundred dollars are now scattered around me across the bed. Confused, I lift my head, turning my glare on the other woman once again. "What—?"

Before I can say more, Emmie is already speaking. "That should cover your cost, yeah? You don't look like you would charge more than that for a few nights in his bed."

"How dare you?" I sputter. Is she really calling me a whore? For real? I went to Yale. I have a degree in journalism, and my parents can buy and sell this girl a hundred times over. She has no right to insinuate I am a whore. "As soon as I tell Shane what you just said to me, you will be gone. Do you hear me? Gone. I won't put up with having you around, little girl."

Green eyes narrow, but she surprises me when she starts to laugh. "Yeah, I've heard that one a time or ten. Go ahead. Try. I bet every dime I just handed over that he doesn't even remember your name."

"Where is Shane?" I demand, so angry I am starting to shake. "I want to talk to him. Now." He will put Emmie Jameson in her place, and then she will be sent packing back to wherever the hell the stupid bitch came from.

Emmie pulls out her phone and waves it at me. "He's probably on the bus by now. He stank to high heaven of nasty skank, so I made him shower." She pushes something on her phone's screen and then hits connect. When I hear the ring of the phone, I know she hit the speaker. My hands fist in the sheet tucked around me as I wait for whomever she's just called to pick up.

"Em?" Shane's deep voice fills the room and makes my tummy do that silly somersault it always does whenever I hear it. Fuck, I love him so much. "Everything okay, honey?"

"Hey. Did you forget to take your trash out again?" Her voice is cool, but I see the spark in her eyes. The affection shining out of those green depths makes my hands start to sweat.

No. He wouldn't. She can't be right. He loves me as much as I love him.

He loves me.

He. Loves. Me.

"Ah, fuck. Em, I'm sorry. I completely forgot the bitch was still there. I thought she would have hit the road by now. Sorry, sweetheart." He blows out a tired breath. "Can you get rid of her for me? I'll love you forever."

Emmie smirks. "Sure. No problem. See you soon."

"Thanks, Em. Love you."

"Love you too." That evil smirk is still on her lips when she disconnects and lifts her eyes to mine. "Good thing you didn't take my bet."

I shake my head, in complete denial. It isn't true. It can't be. Shane loves me. He loves me.

He.

Loves.

Me.

It is all this bitch's fault. Rage boils in my blood. Yes, it is Emmie Jameson's fault. Shane loves me. He loves me, and she is trying to make him give me up. Well, I'm not going to let her. I'll never let her. Shane is mine.

Mine.

A scream fills the air as I jump from the bed, not caring that I am completely naked, and I swing my hands at the redhead. My nails are long—fake, but long. I've used them before in a fight, and my father had to pay the other girl's plastic-surgery bills because I scratched her pretty face up so bad. I will do the same to Emmie. Her beautiful face won't be the same once I get done with her.

Strong hands wrap around my arms, locking them against my body. The second roadie holds me without trouble while Emmie stares dispassionately at me. "Well, good talk. See you never." Tossing her long hair over her shoulder, she turns and walks out of the room as if I don't warrant another thought.

The roadie holds on to me for several minutes without saying a word. Once he's given Emmie enough of a head start, he pushes me down onto the bed and follows her. I sit there, staring at the closed door, hating Ember Jameson more than I've ever hated anyone in my life.

She'll pay.

One day she will pay for taking Shane away from me.

But I can't really think about how I am going to make her pay at this moment. I'm supposed to leave for home soon. I hadn't planned to be going home at all. I had been confident I had accomplished my goal and I would be finishing Shane's tour with him.

And Emmie ruined everything

What am I going to do now? I made a deal with my parents. One I am sure they are going to make me live up to. I don't want a career in journalism. I don't want a career in any field. I want to be taken care of like the queen I am—by Shane Stevenson.

As I sit there contemplating my next move, I hear my cell phone chime, alerting me I have a text message. My heart races, thinking it's Shane texting me that he's sorry for what Emmie made him do. I reach over to the nightstand where I'd put it on the charger the night before after he'd made love to me for the third—or was it the fourth?—time. I will forgive him.

Disappointment hits me when I look at my phone and see it's not from Shane. The text is from Reginald.

Reginald: Good morning, beautiful. When do you return to LA? I'd love to take you to dinner.

I'd told Reginald I was visiting family in Florida for some time before I returned to LA. He didn't need to know I was following the band for a few more shows. I'm glad I told him that. It appears Reginald may just have to be my Plan B.

Me: Hey you. I get in later this evening.

Reginald: May I pick you up from the airport? We can grab dinner.

Me: I would love that. I've missed you. I'll send you my flight itinerary.

May as well start laying on the charm now. I pull up my flight info and send it to him. Shortly after, he responds.

Reginald: I'll meet you at baggage claim. I can't wait to see you.

I could do worse than becoming the wife of *Rock America's* editor. It helps that he owns half of the magazine. Now, to come up with my plan to get him to fall in love with me and marry me, all the while convincing my parents why I shouldn't be held to my end of our deal. Maybe I can tell them my future husband is going to give me a job and then worry about the rest later. I have a six-hour plane ride to figure it all out.

I get out of the bed and head for the shower. I need to get back to my hotel and gather my stuff to make my flight.

FOUR

I have been having the time of my life over the last six months. Reginald and I are in a serious relationship, and with a little pressuring from my parents, he asked me to marry him a couple nights ago. I said yes, but I can't help but think of Shane. Of course, the next day, the news of our engagement was everywhere, and then Shane ended up in the tabloids too. He had been drinking and got into a scuffle with some bar patron. The thing that caught my eye, though, was the female in the shot with him. She had caramel hair and violet-colored eyes. Was he so upset over my engagement that he not only got into a fight, but he latched on to the first woman who turned his head?

Of course, I still love Shane, but Emmie ruined that for us, and I have to settle for a life with Reginald. For now. Although Reginald has been showing me the world, I definitely miss Shane and often think of how our life together would be. What it *will* be like once I eventually divorce Reginald, take half his money, and return to Shane. But that will have to wait a bit longer. My parents are still on my back, and I need to stay off their radar at least until after I've been married a few years. Especially after...everything.

About six weeks after I returned home from my weekend with Shane, I found out I was pregnant. But because I wasn't sure if the baby was Shane's or Reginald's, I had to make the choice to terminate it. It killed a little piece of me to do that, but I just couldn't bring myself to have the baby and run the risk of it being Reginald's. All I have left as proof is a sonogram that I have tucked away. Just one more thing Emmie took from me, took from us. And one more thing that bitch has to pay for.

When she least expects it, though, I will make her pay for it all.

As I am deep in thoughts about what Shane's baby would have looked like, my phone starts buzzing. I pick it up to see Mira's face. She was my roommate in college and is my best friend.

"Hey, girl," I say as I answer the phone.

"And why am I reading on the internet that my best friend is getting married?" she gripes.

"I'm sorry, really. It all happened so fast. My head has not stopped spinning yet." I try to soothe her.

"I swear, Helena, if I didn't know you better, I would think you didn't give a shit about me at all. You've kept some stuff from me in the past, but this takes the cake. Stop being selfish," she continues.

"Mira, I'm sorry," I say again, contrite but still annoyed. "What can I say? You're my only friend. I never really had friends until you. Forgive me," I beg. "Will being my maid of honor make it up to you?"

"Helena, you just said I'm your only friend, so it's a given that I'm going to be your maid of honor," she says with a snort before continuing, and I can hear the excitement in her voice. "Besides, I have my own news I'm excited about."

"Really? What has happened in your world? Have you found yourself a Mr. Right?" I ask. I honestly don't care that she wants her news to outshine mine. Marrying Reginald is really just a means to an end for me. A short detour before my real future starts with Shane.

"Better. I just landed the best job in the universe. I am now a publicist in one of the largest PR firms in the country," she squeals.

"Really? That's awesome news," I respond, trying to keep my boredom from seeping through.

"And guess who one of our largest clients is?"

"You've got me. I have no clue."

"Demon's Wings!" she exclaims.

I almost drop my phone. My best friend is going to have to cover and hide stuff from the tabloids about the best band ever—not to mention, my Shane Stevenson? Oh, this day couldn't get any better.

"Hello? Helena, did you hear what I said?"

"Sorry, Mira, yes. That is awesome news. I am so happy for you," I gush, trying to control how hard my heart is pounding. It *is* awesome news. Amazing, perfect news. Now, I can easily keep up with everything going on in my love's life.

I just have to figure out how to use this to my advantage. My best friend can give me the inside scoop and not even realize she is doing it. I never told her about my weekend with Shane. He is my secret—mine and mine alone—and I don't want to share it or him with anyone. Now...to work on getting information out of her without Mira realizing what I'm doing. This is my in. Not only will I be able to keep tabs on Shane, but this is how I will get my revenge against Emmie Jameson for taking Shane away from me.

"You seem to be deep in thought, Helena." Mira breaks the silence.

"Let's get together soon, Mira. We have a wedding to plan, and I want to hear all about your new job."

"I arrive back in LA next week, so we'll do dinner and drinks when I get there. I'll call you soon."

I hit end on my phone and toss it back on the table.

Mother has put together an engagement dinner for tonight. I swear, any reason to have a dinner party, and that woman is all over it. I dread these kinds of things. I will probably know four people at this event—three of those people share my DNA, and I'm marrying the other one.

I look in the mirror and run my finger over the birthmark on my chin. I hate it. It's not the typical brownish color; it's more red. I wanted to have it removed, but every dermatologist and plastic surgeon my mother took me to advised against it. Over the years, I have learned how to cover it up completely with makeup. But that doesn't mean I like it. It's a pain in the ass, really.

Just as I turn from the mirror, there is a knock at my bedroom door, and I hear my mother's voice.

"Helena, darling. May I come in?"

"Yes, Mother," I call back, and she walks in with a garment bag in her arms.

"Here is your dress for tonight's dinner," she says as she takes it to my walk-in closet and hangs it up.

"Thank you, Mother," I mutter, rolling my eyes behind her back before she walks toward me and wraps her arms around me. Ugh, I hate having to put on a happy face for this woman. If she really knew how much I disliked her, she probably wouldn't dote on me so much. She has been even more over the top since I brought Reginald home to meet them.

"I would like for your father to escort you downstairs this evening, while Reginald waits for you at the bottom of the staircase," she says, unwrapping her arms from around me, outlining her plans for my entrance. That's the thing about my mother. She is all about appearances, and a flashy entrance is high on her priority list.

"Whatever makes you happy, Mother."

"Helena," she scolds. "This is one of the many big events that lead up to your wedding. Please cooperate with me."

"I understand, Mother. But this is my engagement dinner, and I will only know you and Daddy, Sean, and Reginald. This is an event for your friends and Daddy's colleagues. I just don't understand why I have to do this," I whine.

"Because, Helena, your father has a social status that must be maintained, and this is what we do in our world. You'll see. Your future husband has a position in society as well, and you will have to do these events for both him and your future children."

"Please don't start planning children that may or may not happen in my future," I scoff and turn to walk into my bathroom. A shudder runs through me at the thought of having anyone's child but Shane's.

"Helena..." I hear my mother say, but I shut the door to drown out the sound of her annoying voice.

Standing there looking in the mirror, I decide that with this new life, it is time for a change. First, change in hair color. I think strawberry blond will accent my skin tone. Then, this damn birthmark. I may not be able to have it removed, but I'm not walking out my front door without it covered again.

Reginald thinks it's adorable. Who the fuck says that? *Adorable.* He says it makes me unique and I shouldn't worry about it. For a while, I think I was starting to believe him. Looking at it now, uncovered, it is hideous.

I pull out my makeup bag and begin working on making it go away.

I am taking one last look at myself in the full-length mirror in my bedroom when I hear a knock at my door.

"Helena, sweetie, may I come in?" my father asks.

I walk over to the door and open it for him. I had locked it earlier to keep Mother out. I'm grown and do not need her to help me dress or tell me how to do my makeup. I really can't wait to get out of this house. No more daily lectures about where I should go in life, how I should dress for appearance's sake, and all her other bullshit.

"Hi, Daddy."

"Are you ready, sweetie?"

"I am. May I have a minute with you before we head downstairs?" I ask, motioning him to come farther into my room. Once he is standing next to my dresser, I close the door behind him.

"Daddy, I love you. Thank you for escorting me downstairs this evening."

"Sweetie, is something bothering you?"

"I guess I'm a little nervous, that's all." I put a small hitch in my voice, knowing it will get the effect I need.

I know exactly how to wrap my daddy around my finger. If he thinks I'm nervous or anxious, he will keep Mother from making it worse for me.

"Did you take your medicine today?" he asks.

"Yes, Daddy," I lie. I hate taking those damn pills for my bipolar, and I haven't in a long, long time.

He wraps me in a hug. "I'll be right there if you need me tonight. Just give me the signal. You'll always be my little sweetie."

Daddy and I came up with a signal years ago. If I was ever at one of these stupid parties Mother was throwing and I got anxious, I would twirl my hair, and he would stop whatever conversation he was in to come rescue me. I figured out at a young age how to use my illness to my advantage with Daddy.

"Thanks, Daddy," I murmur softly when he releases me and kisses my forehead.

He extends his arm to me, and I place mine in his to take this walk down the staircase. Thankfully, Mother listened to me when I asked for a dress that was only long in the back. My biggest fear has always been tripping over a long dress as I make an entrance.

I have to say, the dress Mother picked for this event is incredibly beautiful. I love how it sits off my shoulders and swoops down to accent my cleavage. And the color, silver with black accent crystals, makes me feel like a diamond worthy of a rocker.

Worthy of Shane.

Daddy and I are standing at the top of the staircase when I take one more last breath to steady myself. I'm not nervous for any reason other than I don't like these things. I wish my mother would just accept it and move on to another reason to throw a party. One that doesn't involve me or even have anything to do with me in general so I don't have to attend the damn things.

Then I see Reginald waiting for me as Daddy and I descend the stairs. He looks so handsome in his black tuxedo with a silver tie. I guess Mother made him coordinate with my dress. Any woman would be lucky to have him as a husband, but for me, he is just a stepping-stone on my path.

We reach the bottom of the staircase, and Daddy hands me off to Reginald.

"You look exquisite, darling," Reginald says as he takes my hand and kisses it gently.

"You do too, my love." I've gotten used to calling him that, but it still makes my stomach clench with distaste at the lie. Shane is my *only* love.

Daddy walks ahead of us, giving us this moment. I hear him announce our entrance to the waiting guests as we walk behind him. Everyone in the large sitting room turns their attention on us as we step inside. We begin to mingle, accepting congratulations from all of Daddy's colleagues. I recognize a few of them from over the years of Mother putting on these stupid dinner parties. I don't know any of them personally and have never wanted to.

Daddy tells the guests that dinner will be served shortly and asks everyone to make their way to the backyard. Mother has had the backyard converted into a dining area just for this evening. It's actually incredibly pretty. The backdrop of the ocean with the twinkling lights hanging from the tented areas gives it an almost magical feel. It makes me long for Shane to be there with me so we could enjoy the beauty of the moment together.

Reginald and I take our seats at the head table, joining Daddy and Mother. Daddy sits to my right, with Mother next to him. He did that to make himself a barrier between Mother and me. I really believe he is always on my side, even though he may not speak up.

I only have to twirl my hair once the whole evening

when Mother is droning on and on over what a lovely bride I am going to make and how she hopes I will quickly start a family. True to form, Daddy comes to my rescue and whisks me away to the dance floor Mother had created directly off the dining area.

"Thank you, Daddy."

"No thanks necessary, sweetie," he says as he twirls me around.

Daddy makes a speech at the end of the night, thanking everyone for coming out to celebrate his beautiful daughter and future son-in-law. Mother is incredibly pleased with the success of the evening. It may come as a shock, but I agree with her. The evening was a success, except for the one thing missing. My Shane. I know he is upset this is one more step that ties me to another man.

Not for long, though. I will make this sacrifice for him. For our future. *I'm always yours, Shane. Always.* I send my silent message to him. *I'll make it up to you.*

FIVE

Mira and I meet for dinner the evening after she arrives back in LA. I am excited to see her. We haven't spent much time together since we graduated. She went back to spend time with her family, and I came back to mine. Then I began my Demon's Wings adventure.

"When do you start this amazing new job as a publicist?" I ask as we sip our cocktails.

"Next week, officially. But I went to the office today to meet everyone and see my office."

"I'm really happy for you. And I'm glad you landed a job that has brought you to LA."

What I'm really glad about is that she has handed me the keys to Demon's Wings so easily. My best friend has no clue just how happy I really am.

"Me too. I've missed hanging out with you."

"Weekly wine nights are a must for us," I say, raising my glass to toast her. Not that I really care about hanging out with Mira on a weekly basis, but it serves a purpose. I will have her talking in no time about the juicy gossip she will have to cover up for Demon's Wings. Most importantly,

Shane. I need to know every detail of his day-to-day, if possible. And hopefully she will give me some dirt on Emmie that I will be able to use to get back at that stupid slut. I ache to ruin her life and make her suffer for every day she has kept me from Shane.

The next few months go by in a whirlwind. Between the planning of my wedding to Reginald, the stress my mother puts me through during the process, and my weekly wine nights with Mira, I am beyond exhausted. I reluctantly started taking my medicine again, just so I can keep up with everything. As much as I hate taking the meds, I knew it was the only way I could get myself through all of this.

But finally, that is all behind me. Reginald and I are married. We honeymooned in Antigua, and for a very brief time, I genuinely felt some sort of happiness—despite missing Shane the whole time and wishing he were beside me instead of my for-now husband. Living the life of a magazine editor's wife has its high points. I travel with Reginald when he has to get behind-the-scenes material of bands.

Life at home with Reginald is quiet. He works long hours at the office, which leaves me to shop or spend the afternoon at the spa. I, along with my parents, convinced him to hire my cousin Sean at the magazine shortly after we got married. Once Reginald proposed, it was easy to get my parents off my back about finding a job. That was when my parents turned their sights on Sean's future since they practically raised him.

Mira has been basically a wealth of useless knowledge for months when it comes to Shane and Emmie. He's been seen out with the same girl the paps spotted him with after my engagement was announced. He looks miserable in the pictures. The smile on his face is about as fake as the girl who is always with him. Fake in the way that no one can be that plain. He is punishing himself for not coming after me. *Soon, Shane. We'll be together again.*

Until the night Mira tells me about him asking the gold digger to marry him.

"Can you believe the manwhore himself is getting married?" Mira exclaims with an annoying giggle. "And she even works for your husband."

I almost choke on the last part. Harper Jones works for Reginald? Why did I not know this?

"She works at *Rock America*?" I ask, keeping my surprise to myself.

"That's what I hear. Actually, I think she just got a promotion and is one of the editors now. Rumor has it she is going to give *Rock America* the inside scoop on the wedding."

"Well, that should be great for sales." I'm at a loss for words.

Shane is going to marry her. That is the ultimate kick in the gut from him. Going out on the town with her, landing on the cover of tabloids, all of that was just Shane acting out for what I had done by marrying Reginald. He must think I have given up on him.

I haven't given up on you, Shane. Just a little bit longer and we will be together.

Somehow, I have got to break up this relationship. And I know the exact person to help me. I pull out my phone and call Sean.

"Hey, cousin. I need your help," I say as I exit my vehicle and walk into my house.

--

When Sean arrives at my house, I greet him at the door. "How come you didn't tell me about Harper Jones working at *Rock America?*" I demand with my hands on my hips.

"I honestly didn't know about her." He huffs. "She has been working in New York and just recently transferred out here. Not to mention, she took my job." He storms past me to enter the house.

"Wait, what are you talking about, she took your job?" I ask as I follow him inside, puzzled by this information.

"Yeah." He turns around, glaring. "I'm her assistant. I thought for sure I was getting the editor's job."

"I'm sorry, Sean. I don't understand how Reginald could do that to you." I hug him. "But still, why didn't you come to me? I would have fixed this and made Reginald give you the job you have worked so hard for."

"Honestly, I've been so upset that I didn't think about coming to you."

"Sean, we have to do something. This little plain Jane is a thorn in my side."

Sean and I walk into the kitchen, and I pour us each a glass of wine.

"We'll handle this together. The whole lot of them won't know what hit them," I say, handing him a glass. "We will bring their lives crashing down around them." We clink our glasses together.

SIX

"Ladies and gentlemen, I give you Mr. and Mrs. Shane Stevenson!"

I sip my glass of champagne, while around me, the lights go out, and a spotlight shines on the dance floor. I press my lips together as Shane Stevenson pulls his new wife into his arms and the first notes of John Legend's "All of Me" fill the air. I watch with a roll of my eyes as Harper's chin trembles before her husband holds her close and they dance their first dance together as husband and wife.

What does he see in that plain little nobody? It's a thought I've had more than once in the last two years. In fact, I've asked myself that from the moment I saw that first picture of the man I loved with his "first girlfriend," as the paps had called her. With her caramel hair that is more on the blond side, her thin body, small chest, and fat ass, she is definitely not the usual type Shane goes for. That's probably the appeal then, I figure.

He is still pissed at me, so he wanted someone as unlike me as he could find. He's succeeded, but fuck, he didn't have to take it this far.

The paps, like always, had gotten it wrong, though. I was Shane Stevenson's first girlfriend, his first love. His *only* love. If it hadn't been for a certain conniving little bitch, Shane and I would still be together, and Harper Jones— Harper Stevenson, now—would never have entered the picture. This would have been *my* wedding, and I never would have had to endure the one my mother made me suffer through to marry Reginald. That would be me out there in that too-beautiful dress being sung to by the drop-dead sexy rocker, his deep voice mixing perfectly with John Legend's.

My drink is empty before the song is even half over, and I take a fresh glass from a waiter who has paused while the bride and groom dance. If you asked me if the wedding had been beautiful, I couldn't have told you. No one but close family and friends were invited to the actual ceremony. The reception, however, is the party to end all parties.

I hadn't been surprised when I'd gotten the invitation in the mail. I'd known from the moment Shane had announced to the world he was marrying his plain mouse of a girlfriend that I would get that little piece of mail. As punishments went, marrying someone else to get back at me was pushing the line, but I could forgive him.

Had forgiven him.

Hell, I could forgive him anything, and he knows it.

He, however, has yet to forgive me for marrying someone else.

But he will.

Eventually.

Shane has been angry. He'd gone wild two years ago when I'd announced my engagement. The tabloids and more reputable weekly magazines had shown him getting drunk on a nightly basis and then getting into a fight at a nightclub. That same night, he'd been spotted with Harper Jones, so I had only myself to blame for their relationship, and I hadn't been upset when the two had become a couple. I'd known he was just trying to get back at me.

Which is exactly what he did today by marrying the little gold-digging nobody slut.

Once again, I remind myself I have no right to get mad or feel hurt, but of course, I am. I hate the thought of him with her, telling her he loves her, maybe even giving her a baby. If they do have a kid before we can get back together, there is no fucking way that kid is going to come to live with us. Harper can keep the little brat, and I will give Shane at least one—maybe two if he begs.

Just like I know my own marriage won't last, I am sure Shane's marriage to Harper won't either. My marriage to Reginald was just to pacify my parents until they died...or he did. At first, I'd thought about divorcing him after a while to appease Mother, but Reginald had made me sign a stupid prenuptial agreement that basically left me with nothing if I were to divorce him. Not that I care about getting anything from him, but my parents had already been bitching when I'd slipped up once and said something about divorce. So unless one of them or Reginald dies first, I am stuck for the moment. But as soon as my parents are gone, I will divorce the man and marry the one I really want—the one I should have been with all along. Shane will do the same when he knows I'm free.

Then we will finally be together.

Like we were supposed to be four years ago.

The lights come back up with the last strings of the song, and my gaze goes past Shane and his bride to the redhead standing just behind them on the edge of the dance floor. Emmie Jameson—now Emmie Armstrong—is standing with a bright smile on her face next to her husband and daughter. For the first time all day, my anger starts to bubble up, and I clench the delicate stem of the champagne flute hard, nearly breaking the expensive crystal.

Time after time, *precious little* Emmie has kept me from being with Shane. It is her fault Shane and I aren't together now, and I will never forgive the conniving little bitch for stepping in our way. Once Shane knows how his adopted little sister has stood in our way, once I am free and tell him how she's kept us apart, I know he won't forgive her either.

That smile will be gone forever from that little cunt's beautiful face. I will never let Shane see her again, not that he will want to once he knows what she did to us.

"You're thirsty this evening, aren't you, darling?"

I force a smile to my lips as I tilt my head back to look up at Reginald. My husband is a very good-looking man, with dark eyes and a slightly sun-kissed complexion. He works out religiously, or I wouldn't be able to stand for him to touch me. But it was his money, and only his money and all those expensive presents he gave me every day, that had tempted me when my parents had started making noises about disinheriting me.

"I am, my love," I murmur with a small smile that I know looks adoring. I'd stood in front of my mirror until I perfected that particular look. The more Reginald thought I loved him, the more money he spent on me. "Do you mind?"

He steps closer and presses a kiss to my temple. "Of course not, darling. Drink as much as you want. Stevenson has pulled out all the stops for Harper."

For the next few hours, I drink as much of the expensive champagne as I can get my hands on and dance with my husband as well as several other guests. I am even gracious enough to pause long enough to congratulate the happy couple.

"Thanks for coming," Harper says to Reginald as she kisses his cheek. "This means a lot to me that you and your wife would be here for us today."

"We wouldn't have wanted to be anywhere else, would we, darling?" Reginald wraps his arm around my waist and smiles charmingly down at me.

"No, of course not. It was an honor to be invited to your wedding reception. Thank you for having us," I murmur, glancing at Harper as she smiles so lovingly up at Shane. "Congratulations to you both."

"Thanks," Shane says with a smirk to me, but I can see the anger blazing out of his eyes. The hurt. The pain. My heart clenches at the sight. *I'm so sorry, my love,* I want to say but don't. *One day,* I promise him with my eyes. *One day, I will make this all up to you.*

After a few more minutes, the couple moves on to speak to their other guests, and I head back to our table with Reginald. While he goes off to get me another glass of champagne, I let my eyes drift to Shane, who is now out on the dance floor with his tiny niece in his arms.

Little Mia Armstrong giggles as her beloved uncle swings her around to the music, singing along with her to the words of the popular pop song the little girl obviously enjoys. Even though I've never really liked children, the sight is cute, and I find myself actually smiling at the two. For a moment, my heart clenches, remembering the baby that might have been Shane's. We would have been a beautiful, happy little family if I could have known for sure the baby was his and not Reginald's.

Shane would make a good father, and for him and only him would I dare to even think about having a child of my own. It would make him happy, so I am sure I will give him a son or daughter. Eventually. I still have a few more years to enjoy my stunning figure before I let him get me pregnant again.

While I continue to watch, I see Emmie gazing adoringly after them, her big green eyes smiling happily at her daughter and adopted brother. The world knows that Emmie worships her daughter, the little creature who is her spitting image.

What, I wonder as my hate for the woman continues to grow with each passing second that I look at her, would Emmie Armstrong do if something happened to that lovely little girl?

--

ON THE RIDE home from the reception, I can't help thinking about what I overheard in the bathroom earlier in the evening. No one knew I was in there. I had gone in to get away from Reginald for a few minutes so I could process my emotions without him watching over me.

Vince Grady, that's the name I heard. He's had Jesse Thornton served with custody papers for little Lucy Thornton. And Layla is beside herself with fear. There had been real distress in her voice as she'd spoken to her sister Lana and Emmie, and I couldn't help smiling as I'd listened to them. Emmie wouldn't like it very much if something happened to someone in her family.

It shouldn't be too hard to find this Vince Grady. I'm sure he needs to make a few dollars. Why else would he come after his child? From what I heard Lana say about him, he doesn't want Lucy; he wants money. Well, I'll contribute if it means some heartache will come to Emmie.

I text Sean.

Me: Hey, cousin. Find me everything you can on Vincent Grady.

Sean is brilliant at locating personal information on the internet.

Sean: Sure thing, Helena. I'll let you know what I find.

I read the message and put my phone in my clutch, hiding a grin.

"Everything okay, darling?" Reginald asks from the driver's seat.

"Just Sean checking in."

A couple days later, I'm sitting in front of a run-down motel, waiting for Vince Grady to exit his room. I have ten thousand dollars in cash with me, and by the looks of this place, in the middle of drug central, I'm sure this guy will do what I want. Ten thousand dollars will buy him a lot of drugs.

Just as I'm about to give up, I see him leaving his room. I get out of my car and walk toward him.

"Mr. Grady?" I call to him. He turns around.

"Who's askin'?" he questions.

"That doesn't matter. What does matter is that I'm here to help you."

"Sorry, darlin', not sure what you can do to help me," he grunts back.

"Let's just say I can get you closer to your goal of wreaking havoc on the Demon's Wings family. They have your daughter Lucy, right?"

"I don't want the brat." He spits on the ground between us. "I want the money she will bring me."

"I get that. But in the process, I want you to inflict some

pain on the redhead they call Emmie. I'm willing to pay you."

"Who the fuck are you, lady?" he asks.

"It doesn't matter who I am. Do you want my money or not?" I demand.

"I like money. What is it you want me to do to this redhead?"

"The redhead will be taking Lucy to a friend's house tonight for Halloween." I begin to lay out the details Sean acquired from an unwitting Harper. "Follow her, and when the moment presents itself, take the kid. She will fight to protect Lucy," I continue. "And really, I don't care what you do to the redhead—beat her within an inch of her life, if you so choose. Rape her if that's what gets you off. Just show no mercy."

"Seems you've thought this out for me."

"I don't care what you do with the child, but it will probably get you the money you want if you kidnap her after you handle Emmie. They will pay just about anything to get the kid back."

I hand him the envelope with the cash in it. But before releasing it, I make my point clear.

"Do not mention this conversation to anyone. Here is the first payment. I will keep giving you money as long as you never mention me to anyone, and you continue to wreak havoc on the redhead." I release the envelope and turn to walk away.

"Oh, and one other thing." I turn back around and make eye contact with him. "I have eyes everywhere. Don't follow through, and there will be no more cash coming your way."

I quickly head back to my rented vehicle, get in, and drive away.

As soon as I am in traffic, I hit connect on my headset.

"Sean, I've handled what I needed to with Vince Grady. I want you to follow Emmie tonight to make sure he does what I just paid him to do."

Sean agrees, and I press end on my phone and head to the gym. I feel the sudden urge to get a workout in, but it will also be a cover for the clothes I have on if Reginald gets home before I do.

SEVEN

"Emmie and her new baby are fine now," Mira confides as we sip our wine in my living room.

"What happened to the guy who assaulted her and kidnapped Lucy?" I ask, trying to hide my disgust that Emmie is pregnant again.

"Not sure. All Emmie said was the police have Vince Grady in custody."

What a fucking moron, I think to myself as I take another sip of wine.

Emmie is pregnant again, Lucy is safe and sound with Jesse and Layla, and Vince Grady is in custody.

Oh shit! Vince Grady is in custody. What if he mentions the mystery woman? I jump up from the couch in a panic.

"I totally forgot. I have an appointment!" I exclaim. "Sorry to cut our wine afternoon short."

Mira stands up, and I take her wineglass from her.

"Helena, are you okay?" she asks as I shuffle her to the front door.

"I'm fine. I just forgot about a meeting with Mother.

You know how she gets when I'm late." I rush to cover my panic.

Once I see Mira pull out of the driveway, my emotions get the better of me. I begin smashing everything in sight. Knocking vases full of beautiful flowers off tables, shattering pictures of Reginald and me, pulling items off the shelves.

"That bitch has everything!" I scream.

By the time Reginald gets home from work, I am in the fetal position in the middle of the floor, shattered glass all around me.

"Helena!" he exclaims, rushing to me and picking me up in his arms. "Darling, talk to me," he insists.

I have nothing to say to him. I just lie there in his arms, looking off into the distance. I feel him shift to get his cell phone out of his pocket.

"I need an ambulance!" I hear him say into the phone. It sounds like I'm underwater for the rest of his conversation. I've checked out.

--

When I wake up, I'm in a dark hospital room. I can see Reginald sleeping in a chair next to me. I have no idea what time it is or how long I have been asleep. My arms are stinging with pain. I run my hands over them, and the hand with the IV stuck in it protests as I feel a tug against the bandaging.

"Shit!" I cry out from the pain.

Reginald wakes with a startle at my cry.

"Darling, are you okay?" he asks and moves next to me.

"What happened?" I ask. "Why am I here?"

"You had some sort of meltdown. I came home to find you on the floor, bleeding from all the glass you shattered. Do you not remember?"

"I don't know what happened." I murmur. *Yes, I do. My*

world is falling apart.

Reginald leans in and kisses my forehead. "We'll get you feeling better, darling. The doctor thinks you may need a change in your medication."

"I don't want to take medicine, Reginald," I spit out. "It makes me feel bad."

"Let's try a new one, then. Maybe it won't make you feel that way."

"I'm sorry you have to see me like this," I sob. "You probably hate me." *I couldn't really care less if he hates me. But I still need him.*

"I could never hate you, darling. I love you."

--

It's been a few months since my breakdown. Reginald has been hovering over me to the point of irritation. It's almost like he is afraid to leave me alone. He has even been working from home a lot lately. Last night, I asked him to go back to work.

I'm lying in our bed, and I hear the shower running in our bathroom. Thankfully, he is doing what I have asked him to do.

Without him here, I won't have to take these damn pills anymore. They are worse than the other ones I was on. All I need is my Shane. Once I get him back and we live our forever, I won't need medication. I don't need anything or anyone but him to feel good.

And without Reginald at home hovering over me, I can go back to planning how to get rid of these two bitches who are standing in my way.

Sean has told me he's read Harper's emails, and she is trying to get pregnant with the help of some foreign doctor. She is trying to trap my Shane into staying with her. I have to rescue him.

EIGHT

Thanks to Mira, I know where Demon's Wings are going to be for the next few stops of their tour. I convinced Reginald I need a few days at a spa to get my head together. I even started a few arguments with him so he could see I need some time alone. He claims he is worried about me.

The only thing wrong with me is I am continuing to watch my life from the sidelines.

Another woman is living *my* life.

Touring with Shane, warming his bed. Loving him as I should be loving him.

I am going to destroy her and Emmie and get my life back. I have got to stop Harper from manipulating Shane into staying with her by getting pregnant. I cannot believe Shane is allowing her to go to these lengths. He has to know that I will give him as many children as he wants. I am not going to be with Reginald much longer. I haven't figured out if it will end by divorce or his death, but it is about to end—that, I know for sure.

I have let Emmie and Harper stand in my way long enough. I am going to put an end to them once and for all.

I grab the press badge I still have from the first night I spent with Reginald and pack it in my bag. I knew I kept this around for a reason. This will definitely come in handy for my little adventure. I'll just flash it and get myself back-stage and into crew areas where the buses will be parked.

I walk downstairs with my luggage to find Reginald in the sitting room.

Placing my bags at the foot of the staircase, I call out to him, "I'm getting ready to leave."

"Darling, let me drive you," Reginald says as he walks toward me.

"No!" I half shout and immediately regret it when I see the startled look on his face. I try to rein in my annoyance and anger. Really, I'm fed up with him and this entire rela-tionship. I want to be with Shane so badly, and Reginald is just one more obstacle standing in my way. I've been researching ways to kill someone and make it look like an accident, but so far, nothing is even remotely believable for my husband's sudden death, not without making me appear guilty. "I'm sorry, my love. I just feel out of sorts. I've burdened you enough."

"You're not a burden to me. I'm just worried about you," he says, reaching out for me to engulf me in a hug.

I lay my head on his shoulder and pat him on the back even as I imagine thrusting a knife deep between his shoulder blades and just walking away while he bleeds out on the newly cleaned carpets. "I know the last couple months have been really rocky. I don't know what is wrong with me," I cry.

I do know what is wrong with me. I hate this life. I want the life I was supposed to have with Shane. I'm watching and hearing about some plain Jane living the life I deserve, the one I crave with the man who was meant for only me.

"It's all going to be okay, darling. You'll go get some rest at the spa, and when you get home, you'll feel refreshed." He kisses my forehead.

"Maybe we'll talk about starting a family." I step out of his arms and look up at him, knowing it will make him more amenable. I can pretend a little longer. Just until I can finally get Harper and Emmie out of my Shane's life.

"That would be amazing. But only when you're ready."

I turn, grab my suitcase handle, and walk to the front door. Reginald is walking behind me. I stop before opening the door and turn back to face him.

"Sean is here to pick me up. I'll see you in a few days." The look on his face is one of utter defeat. But he doesn't say a word. I turn back around, open the door, and get in the waiting car. Sean grabs my suitcase and places it in the trunk, waves at Reginald, then climbs back into the driver's seat without a word to my husband. I face forward as Sean drives away, but I can still practically feel Reginald standing in the doorway, watching as we leave.

After a few moments of silence, Sean starts asking questions.

"Cousin, are you sure this is what you really want to do?"

"Yes, Sean, it is. I'm going to get back what's mine. I can't do this anymore."

"But do you have to go to such extreme measures?" He shoots me a bewildered glance. "I mean, the plan you have laid out is kinda scary. I'm not even going to sugarcoat it."

"I know what I'm doing. Shane feels like he is trapped with that simpleton. If she does get pregnant, then he will be stuck with her even longer. But I'm going to fix everything for him—and for me."

"What if you get caught?" Sean asks.

"I'm not going to get caught. I have thought of every single detail," I remind him. "Besides, you're the only other person who knows my plan, and I pay you very well to keep your mouth shut."

"I know, cousin. I know. I just worry about you if this doesn't go as planned."

"It will." We drive the remainder of the way in silence.

Sean checks us in to our hotel room that is just a couple miles away from the venue. I have already covered my bases with Mira, making sure she is not going to be at the show tonight. She thinks the same thing as Reginald, that I am at a spa for the weekend. She is actually traveling to Michigan to spend some time with her family.

We walk into our hotel room, nothing like what I'm used to staying at, but it will do. Two queen beds, a desk, a bathroom, and a closet. I don't want to think about how dirty this room might really be, but this is the kind of place where no one will ask unnecessary questions. Thankfully, Sean is more like a brother than even a cousin. He's the sibling I always wanted but was thankful I never had because I don't like sharing. We spent many nights sleeping in the same room when we were younger.

I put my stuff down and plop onto the bed by the window.

"I need five minutes, and then I'll get myself ready," I say, throwing my head back onto the pillow.

Sean puts his bag down and sits down on the other queen-sized bed.

"Five minutes is about all you have if you are going to keep your schedule."

"Yes, Daddy," I say sarcastically.

"No need for the attitude, I'm just trying to keep you on track. Isn't that what you pay me to do?" he snips back.

After my five minutes of rest, I get up and go into the bathroom with my clothes to change into—a dark hoodie, black yoga pants, and tennis shoes. I had Sean buy me this sweatshirt a couple sizes too big so I could hide my face a little better with it. I'm not going to cover my birthmark. I look like a different person when it isn't covered, because that seems to be all anyone sees. So just in case something goes wrong or I run into Harper, she won't recognize me. I pull my hair back into a ponytail and take one final look in the mirror.

"I'm ready," I say to Sean as I return to the bedroom.

"Cousin, I'm going to ask you one more time. Is this what you really want to do?"

"Sean, how many different ways do I need to say it to you, huh? I'm. Taking. Back. What. Is. Mine!" I scream at him.

"Okay, okay." He pales and practically cowers away, putting his hands up in surrender. "Let's get this over with, then."

We take the back stairs out of the hotel to the parking lot, where we get in Sean's car and head to the venue. I have a small black backpack with me which holds my black gloves, press pass, and a knife.

Flashing my credentials, I make my way around to the area where the buses are parked. I see Harper and another woman I don't recognize leaving a bus and figure it's Shane's. I can hear Demon's Wings onstage in the distance. This is my chance. I'll sneak onto the bus and wait for Harper to return.

I duck onto the bus and look around. It smells like Shane, but I catch a hint of the perfume I know Harper wears. The mixed scents remind me that it should be my perfume meshed with Shane's, not that stupid plain cow's, and I see red. I destroy everything in my path. Breaking mirrors, shattering glasses, jerking the TV off the wall. Taking out my knife, I begin slashing the chairs and couches. I walk back to the sleeping area, but suddenly from behind me, I hear a dog growl.

Oh shit. I wasn't expecting them to bring their dog on tour.

The dog keeps creeping toward me, growling more and more aggressively. As the dog lunges forward in an attempt to attack me, I stab it on instinct to protect myself. That menacing growl is now a pathetic whimper. I slice it one more time, taking my anger and pain out on the dog, when it is really Harper I wish I were stabbing, watching almost in a daze as its blood flows out and around me.

Take that, you fucking mutt. Next time, I promise myself. *Next time, I'll do this to Harper. And that fucking cunt Emmie.*

I kneel next to the ugly thing; it's barely breathing. I dip my glove in its blood and write a warning on one of the mirrors. "You're next, bitches." I step back over the dog, kicking it in the ribs before looking to the front of the bus. With all that growling and whimpering, someone was bound to have heard me.

It's time to abort this plan. My heart is racing, but I feel a weird sense of euphoria as I rush back toward the door. As I hurry away from the bus, I take off the gloves and put them back in my bag, pulling out my cell phone to call Sean. He picks up on the first ring.

"I didn't plan for the fucking dog," I huff.

"Harper didn't mention they were taking the dog on tour," he mutters.

"Well, they did. I stabbed it. Hopefully it will be dead by the time they find the fucking thing."

Just then, I hear a commotion coming from where I just was at Shane's bus. I keep the phone to my ear, but I maneuver myself behind another bus so I can see what is going on but not be noticed.

"Hold on, Sean. I think I see someone at Shane's bus." Just as I say the words into the phone, more people go running toward the bus.

"Cousin, get out of there before you get spotted." I hear Sean saying.

"Shh! I want to see Shane." Just as I say his name, the OtherWorld guitarist runs off the bus with the dog in his arms, and Shane appears. He looks good, and I ache to touch him, but then I hear him scream before both rockers are running to find help for the dog.

"I'm on my way to you, Sean," I say and end the phone call.

I begin a fast-paced walk to the spot in the back parking lot where I told Sean to wait for me. Once I get past the gate, I begin jogging to Sean's car.

"Fuck!" I yell as I get into the passenger seat of the car, and Sean drives off.

"Fuck! Fuck! Fuck!" I continue to shout as I punch the dashboard.

"Calm down, cousin."

"This was a very well-laid-out plan, and your one little screw-up by not telling me about the fucking dog just ruined it, you dumbass!" I scream at him.

"I can't give you information that I don't get myself," Sean protests.

"What's done is done." I hit the dashboard one more time, my hands aching. Shit, my knuckles are bleeding. Now I'll have to come up with a lie to tell Reginald to cover myself. Double fuck! "Just take me back to the hotel. I need to get the mutt's blood off me."

NINE

A few days later, Sean drops me off at my house, and I am angrier than I was when I left. What in the fuck is wrong with the universe? It's been two days since I stabbed the dog and wrecked Shane's bus. Not the plan I had when I left here.

The news of Shane's bus is all over TV and social media platforms. Because of that, I know Reginald won't be home. He is doing his best to get the most current information from the Demon's Wings camp and keep the *Rock America* website, social media, and magazine itself up-to-date. Because of little Harper, my husband gets the only in-depth scoop and reports the facts the tabloids tend to leave out. This will give the magazine huge sales and keep Reginald out of my way for a little while at least.

He texted me earlier to tell me he would be at the office when I returned home. I don't give a fuck. It's better this way. I have to show him I look and feel refreshed, all the while I'm mad as hell on the inside that I didn't succeed with my plan.

As I'm walking into the house, my phone buzzes, and I see it's Mira calling me.

"Hi, Mira," I say cheerfully, seething internally. "How was Michigan?"

"I had to cut my time short to head to Demon's Wings' latest stop on the tour. Did you hear about Shane's bus and his dog?"

"Reginald told me about it. How sad," I say, rolling my eyes. *How sad the fucking dog didn't die.*

"Shane and Harper are devastated. But thankfully, Ranger is going to be okay," she continues. "They love him like he is their own child. And since she can't have kids, I guess he is her little fur baby."

I have to remind myself that no one else knows that Harper had received potentially good news from the latest fertility specialist she'd seen in Germany. Apparently not even Emmie knew that little detail, from what Sean told me when he went through Harper's emails and came across that tiny tidbit of information. Information that is still making me quake with rage.

"Do they know who would do this?" I ask her, masking my anger.

"They have no idea. No one saw anyone or anything out of the ordinary. But thankfully, Emmie is putting cameras on all the buses. Especially the entrances. If this psycho does it again, hopefully they will get caught."

"I can't imagine what they must be going through." I'm getting bored with this conversation, but at the same time, I need to hear what else Mira has to say. She may give me a nugget of information I can use.

Mira mentioning cameras on the buses gives me an idea about putting some of my own cameras in places. I make a mental note to discuss having cameras installed in Emmie's and Harper's houses later.

"It's very rough for all of them. Especially with all the kids traveling with them. Security has been increased for the remaining tour dates."

Well, there is another piece of information I need to have. The next time, my press badge might not work. I'll have to get Sean on the task of figuring it out.

"I'm sorry, Mira," I lie. "I'm sure this chaos is making your life hell right now."

"It definitely is. I just can't believe there is a sick person walking the streets—"

"I've got to go," I cut her off before she pisses me off to the point I slip up and say something I shouldn't. The fucking bitch doesn't know shit. "I just arrived back home today, and I have so much to deal with. Talk soon."

I press end on the call. She just called me a sick person. I am *not* sick. No one understands what Emmie took from me. Not to mention what Harper is keeping from me.

I walk into the kitchen to get a bottle of water.

What am I going to do now?

How do I fix this?

I'm pacing back and forth in the kitchen when Reginald walks in, startling me.

"Welcome home, darling," he says, wrapping his arms around me.

"Hello, my love."

"Would you like me to take you out to dinner tonight?" he suggests.

"Yes, that sounds wonderful." I force a smile. *Not.*

"How was your spa visit?" he asks, releasing me from his arms.

"Not as invigorating as I thought it would be." I shrug. "But it was productive."

That's not a lie. It was productive. I turned their worlds upside down—score one for me—and even if I didn't get to take out Harper, I got their attention.

Hours later, Reginald and I are sitting in Hell's Kitchen. He pulled one of his favors, knowing I have always wanted to come here. My husband genuinely loves and cares for me. I want for nothing. But I don't love him. Can't love him. Nothing will make me forget about the only man I could ever love.

Shane is my forever.

I'm sitting there lost in my thoughts about Shane when I feel the hair stand up on the back of my neck. Did Reginald just ask me about children and if we can start a family? I couldn't have heard that right.

"I'm sorry, my love. What was that you asked about?" I inquire.

"Children, darling. Babies. Can we begin to start our family?" he asks again, looking hopeful.

Shit! He wants to talk about a damn family now? I don't want a family with *him*. I excuse myself from the table and head to the ladies' room, leaving him with a confused look on his face. I do not want to have this conversation. He ruins everything. What about me and what I want?

I get my thoughts together and head back to the table, standing next to my chair. "I don't feel well. Take me home."

"Darling?" Standing, he reaches for me.

"I want to go home, Reginald. You've ruined my appetite. I just wanted to come and have a nice dinner," I spit out.

"I'm sorry, darling. Let's sit and enjoy our meal," he

pleads. *Fuck, why does he have to sound so whiny? It only gives me a headache.*

"Take me home! Now!" I shout, causing other patrons to look at us. I hear them begin to whisper to each other, and I know they are talking about us. "Now, Reginald," I command again when he just stands there looking dumbfounded.

When he doesn't move, I turn around and walk out of the restaurant. I'm leaving with or without him, I really don't care which. He catches up to me as I step outside, grabbing my arm to stop me. I spin around, looking at him with all of the hate and disgust I have brewing inside me.

"Let. Go. Of. Me!" I scream, causing the valet attendant to rush over.

"Is everything okay, ma'am?"

"My wife is fine," Reginald answers before I can, pulling out his parking ticket and handing it over to him.

The young man reluctantly leaves to retrieve our car. Reginald and I stand there in silence until the car is pulled to a stop in front of us. My husband opens my door and I get inside, while he tips the valet and gets behind the wheel.

We are halfway home before Reginald breaks the silence.

"Darling, would you like to tell me what happened back there?"

"You!" I snap back at him. "You are what happened."

"Clearly, you are upset about something I've said. Please, talk to me, and let's work it out," he begs.

"I don't want to talk to you right now. I don't even want to look at you. Just drive me home, and when we get there, leave me alone."

He pulls the car into our driveway. Before he cuts off the engine, I'm out of the car and running into the house.

He makes me so angry. I just want him gone. Out of my life, so I can start my real forever with Shane.

I'm heading up the stairs when I hear him following behind me.

"Helena, stop and talk to me. Please."

I whip around to face him. "*I. Do. Not. Want. To. Talk. To. You!*" I scream in his face.

"Are you acting like this because I asked about starting a family?"

"*Arrrrrrhhhhhhh!*" I scream louder and begin hitting him with my fists. "*Leave me alone. Stop talking! Just fucking stop!*"

He tries to protect himself from my blows, but I just keep pounding on him, letting out all of the aggression I have built up from not succeeding in my plan to get Shane back. All the rage I have built up because I am tired of living this lie.

TEN

Getting into the tour bus area even with all the heightened security is easier than I thought it would be. It is dimly lit back here because some of the lights on the poles are out.

I see Shane's bus. Looking around to make sure no one has noticed me, I open the door and climb aboard. I don't see any sign of the mutt this time. I begin tearing the bus apart like a madwoman. Slicing cushions on the couch and chairs, pulling things off the tables and scattering them along the floor. I walk into the bathroom and take out my red lipstick to write a message on the mirror. *One bitch down. One to go. You're next, you dirty slut.* Then I shatter the mirror with the butt of my gun.

I go back to the front of the bus, feeling a little déjà vu. I turn back to look at my handiwork.

I look out the window to make sure no one is around before I make my exit. Once out of the bus, I take off running back toward the parking lot.

As I'm rushing past the other buses, I see the door to one open and a little girl emerge from it. Mia. Emmie and Nik's little brat. Well, she wasn't part of my plan tonight, but now I've just found my way to destroy her bitch of a mother.

Mia shuts the door to the bus and starts sprinting toward the stage area. The festival is shutting down, with Demon's Wings closing the show, so there aren't many people milling about since they are either watching the band or getting ready to head out to their next stop. The few that are around are roadies packing up the other bands that played tonight. No one seems to notice the small child running like her life depends on it.

I follow her and slowly close the distance between myself and the little girl. When I am satisfied no one is watching, I grab her arm. She screams, and I throw her over my shoulder and hurry toward the exit. She is a squirmy little thing. The harder I hold her, the harder she tries to get out of my grasp. She begins yelling, "Let me go!", hitting my back with her little fists, and kicking her feet.

Fuck. The little monster has the spunk of her mother.

I begin running, tightening my hold to make sure I don't drop her. When I reach the alley, I stop and put my hand over her mouth before taking off again. I make it to the parking lot and run onto the side street outside the stadium where Sean is supposed to be waiting for me.

From behind me, I heard a woman's voice calling Mia's name. Freezing, I stop and glance over my shoulder to see who it could be. It isn't Emmie or any of her aunts, but some little dark-haired woman I don't recognize, so I keep moving.

But the bitch actually starts running after me. She is fast, despite how short she is, and catches up to me before I even realize it. She pushes me from behind, causing me to fall and bring Mia down too. Mia begins to squirm underneath me and tries to crawl away. I jump to my feet and turn toward the female who has been chasing me.

"Mia?" The woman is out of breath but rushes forward and lifts Mia into her arms. "Are you okay, sweetheart?" I hear her ask the little monster.

"I-I w-want my m-m-momma," the annoying brat cries against her chest.

I step in front of the woman. She is not going to ruin this for me. I am so fucking close to destroying Emmie Armstrong's entire world. All I need is to take her daughter, and Emmie's entire life will crash and burn around her. "I don't think so, bitch," I snarl. "You aren't messing this up for me."

I pull the gun Sean had reluctantly gotten for me, which I have hidden my hoodie pocket. My plan had been to shoot Harper since the knife had been too messy when I'd used it on that damn dog. Fingers shaking from my rage, I point it at Mia's would-be savior.

The woman holding Mia stills, staring at me as horror fills her eyes. I pull the trigger, unloading two rounds straight into her chest. I watch as she falls to the ground, taking the child with her.

The shot echoes around me, hurting my ears, and I know someone must have heard it.

Fuck. I've got to get out of here.

I take off running toward where Sean is parked, waiting for me. I swing the door open and jump inside, slamming it once I'm seated.

"Go, go, go!" I scream at Sean as I glance around frantically to make sure no one is watching or following us.

He puts the car in gear and squeals out of the space.

"What the hell happened?" he demands as he speeds onto the interstate.

"I had the little monster in my arms and some bitch stopped me, so I shot her."

"What?" he screeched. "Who the fuck did you shoot, Helena?"

"I don't know. She wasn't anyone related to Mia, but she knew who Mia was."

"Is she dead?"

"Probably. I unloaded two rounds into her chest." I shrug. That bitch better be dead, or I will have to go back and finish her off.

"Helena!" he bellows and pulls the car over.

"What the fuck are you doing, Sean? Drive. Do you not hear the sirens coming?" I demand, noticing he is actually shaking. What a little pussy.

"You shot someone, Helena," he whispers, his eyes full of fear and disgust.

"And? Are you trying to get us caught?"

"Us?" he cries, his face as pale as death.

"Yeah, asshole. Us!" I scream back at him. "Drive. Now!"

After a few tense moments, he finally pulls back onto the interstate and heads south to get us back to LA.

After about an hour of tense driving, Sean speaks again.

"Helena, what do we do now?" he asks, his voice shaking.

"We drive home," I respond nonchalantly with a careless shrug.

"Do you not realize the severity of what you just did? Are you seriously that deranged?" he asks, disgust thick in his tone.

"Listen here, you little shit. I pay you to do what I want, not question me about what I do. Drive this fucking car and get me home." His whining is getting on my nerves.

After all I've done for him, he is being such a little pussy now.

"I'm getting sick of you throwing it in my face that you pay me—"

"I don't give a rat's ass what you are sick of. You want to know what *I'm* sick of?" I ask, looking directly at him. His jaw clenches, and I think I see tears in his eyes. "I am sick of incompetence. I am sick of my plans not going as they should. And most of all..." I turn back to look out the windshield. "I am sick of not having the life I was supposed to have," I say coldly.

"I'm sorry, cousin," he says softly, fear lacing his words. "We'll...figure something out."

He continues to drive, only stopping once for gas and for me to change my clothes. I apply make-up to cover my birthmark as he drives. He pulls into my driveway and cuts the engine. We told Reginald we were going down to one of Sean's friend's houses in San Diego for the day. It's late by the time we get back, but Reginald has no reason to be suspicious.

"Do you want me to come in with you?" he asks hesitantly.

"Yes, I would like that." I open my door. "You can stay in one of the guest rooms," I say as we climb out of the car.

We walk into the house to find Reginald watching TV in the living room.

"Hello, my love."

Reginald gets up from the couch and walks over to me, wrapping his arms around me.

"Oh, darling. I'm so glad you are home." He kisses my forehead. "Someone attacked Gabriella Moreitti tonight at the rock festival upstate."

"Oh my goodness! That's awful," I cry.

"What has the news said about the incident?" Sean asks, and I shoot him a glare to tell him to shut his fucking mouth.

"Apparently, someone was trying to kidnap Mia Armstrong, and Gabriella stopped them."

"That poor baby girl. Emmie must be beside herself," I say, doing my best to be as sincere as possible, when in reality, I couldn't care less. I'm still beyond pissed that Moreitti ruined everything.

"I've spoken to Mira. Shane and Harper's bus was destroyed again, too," Reginald continues, shaking his head.

"That is awful. Have you spoken to Harper?" I ask.

"Not yet. I've left a message for her, but I'm sure right now isn't the best time to talk to her."

"I'm going to head to the guest room. That drive was pretty long," Sean interrupts, changing the subject.

"See you in the morning, Sean," I say as he leaves the living room.

"Good night, Sean," Reginald calls out to him.

I head upstairs to my bathroom to get in the shower and wash the stench of the day off of me. As I am standing under the spray of the hot water, I begin to cry. Sliding down the wall, I just let it all out. Another failed plan. Another night without my Shane.

ELEVEN

I arrive at the restaurant to meet Mira for lunch. As I am being seated, my phone dings, alerting me I have a text message.

Mira: Running a couple minutes behind. I'll be there shortly.

Me: Okay. I'm at the table. Hope everything is okay.

Mira arrives about twenty minutes after her text. There's really nothing new she can tell me about Demon's Wings—or Shane, for that matter.

Our lunch arrives, and we eat, talking about the meaningless shit she is working on for some of her other clients.

From lunch, I head to my parents' house. The items I need for the hell I'm about to bring to Harper are in the secret hiding place I have in my old room. I couldn't run the risk of Reginald ever finding these things. I really didn't think about using them to destroy Harper until now. These items are sacred to Shane and me.

"Hello, sweetie." My daddy greets me with a kiss on my forehead when I arrive.

"Hi, Daddy."

"I wish I'd known you were coming over. Your mother is out shopping."

"It's okay, Daddy. I just wanted to see you. I've missed you."

"I've missed you too, sweetheart."

I don't see my daddy as often as I would like to, especially lately with everything I have on my plate trying to get my life with Shane back.

"Actually, Daddy, I need to pick up a few things I left in my room," I say as I walk to the staircase.

"Sure, sweetheart. I'll be in my study. Come say goodbye before you leave."

"I will. I promise."

I open the door to my room. Mother hasn't changed anything; it still looks like it did the day I moved in with Reginald. I walk over to the closet and pull the board from the back of the built-in shoe rack. I created this hiding place when I was a teenager. I reach my hand inside and remove the envelope stored there.

I sit on the floor and open it, pulling out the pictures I haven't let myself look at in years. Shane has no clue I even took these. He was so lost in the moment when he was making love to me that he didn't notice I was snapping pictures on my phone. At the time, I was taking them so we could reminisce about our first time together as we celebrated milestones in our relationship.

These pictures take me back to that weekend—when we consummated our love. I wipe away a tear as I look through them, remembering each touch, each word he said to me. He must have been so pissed at me to try to hurt me like he did when he told Harper she was his only love. I don't know how I am going to make it up to him, but I promise I will.

Then I come across the sonogram that is the last picture in the stack. I sit there for several minutes looking at it.

I put everything back in the envelope, stand up, and leave my room, shutting the door behind me.

"I'm leaving, Daddy." I peek my head in his study. He sits at his desk, busily working away.

"I love you, sweetheart."

"I love you too, Daddy," I say, shutting his door and heading out of the house.

I'm sitting in Sean's apartment when he arrives home from work.

"Hey, cousin," he greets me, but I see caution on his face. He's been acting differently ever since the whole Mia-Gabriella mishap.

"I need you to make copies of these." I point to the envelope sitting on his coffee table. Everything but the ultrasound picture is in there. I'm not ready to share my baby with anyone else yet, but I will if Harper makes me.

He walks over and picks it up, taking the photos out.

"Good God, Helena!" he gasps. "A little notice before letting me see something like this. Fuck!"

"Get over it, Sean. It's not like you've never seen porn."

"Who is this?" he asks, setting the photos down.

"It's Shane and me," I say with a shrug.

"Are you fucking kidding me?" he exclaims. "You've been sitting on these all this time?"

I shrug again. "Make copies and get them in front of Harper," I say as I get up from the couch and cross to the front door before turning back to look at him. "Oh, and don't lose my copies, or you'll regret it. Let me know when you plant them. I want to be at Rock America when Harper gets them." I want to watch her reaction in the flesh rather than on the live feed from the camera in her office. This is going to be perfection, and I can't wait to watch her world fall apart when she realizes Shane is all mine.

"Of course you would. Give me a few days. I'm going to need to figure out how and where to plant them that doesn't tie it back to me."

"You're smart. You'll figure out something." I pause with my hand on the doorknob. "Oh, and one more thing."

"What else would you like me to do for you, cousin?" he asks with a sigh.

"Don't screw this up. Like I said, you're smart. Figure it out. It's probably best if they calm down a little bit after today's good news of Harper not being able to conceive. Then once they think they are all clear from drama, they'll get hit with this."

Some time goes by, but Sean does exactly what I asked him to do. The hardest part of these cameras is watching Shane have sex with Harper. The other houses bore me. I don't give a shit about what they do. I only wanted cameras there to keep tabs on them.

It's Monday morning, and Sean just texted me that he has planted the photos in Harper's office. I make my way to Rock America. I want to be there when she opens the envelope and her world comes crashing down around her. When I arrive, the office is pretty empty. I walk into Reginald's office, surprising him.

"Hi, darling. What brings you here?" he asks.

"I was in the neighborhood and wanted to come kiss my husband," I say, walking over to him.

He wraps me in a hug, and I kiss him passionately, which takes every bit of strength I have, if I'm being honest.

"What a nice surprise," he says as he pulls back from our kiss.

"I know I've been emotional lately and, my love, I am truly sorry." I pout up at him.

"We'll get through it," he assures me. "All marriages have rough patches."

I lean in to kiss him again, when we hear a commotion down the hall.

"I'll be right back. Stay here," he commands.

Reginald leaves his office, closing the door behind him. I walk over to the window that looks out on the corridor and see that Harper has found her prize. I smile to myself. This will surely end their relationship once and for all, and I will have my Shane back.

I'm not sure how much time passes, but then I see Emmie coming down the hallway. I can't hear her, but I can tell that she is barking orders at everyone. Sometime after that, I see the blonde married to Axton arrive. I can't help but be pleased with my handiwork. Poor Harper is losing her shit. Everyone is coming in to save her.

I hear him before I see him. Shane has now arrived. I want to walk out of Reginald's office to wrap my arms around him and let him know I've saved him from her and we can finally be together. But Reginald comes back into his office.

"Darling, it's kind of crazy around here right now. Let's get you out of here, and I'll see you at home later."

I want to protest, but instead, I let him lead me down the back hallway to the elevators.

--

. . .

"WHAT THE FUCK do you mean, Shane and Harper left together?" I seethe.

"The cameras were found too," Sean replies in a meek voice.

"Are you that incompetent?" I scream in his face.

"Cousin, stop. Why don't you just give this up?" he suggests. "Shane and Harper are *not* going to split up. She's manipulated him too much at this point."

"*Yes. They. Will!*" I continue yelling at him. "I don't know what you are doing to fuck this up for me, but you better stop!"

"Me?" he yells back, suddenly seeming to grow a backbone. "I have done everything you have asked me to do to interfere with these people. I have even been demoted because Harper no longer thinks I am competent enough to be her assistant."

"I guess that is one thing she and I have in common, then," I sneer. "I'm done with you for right now. I can't even bear to look at you."

I walk out of Sean's apartment and head to my car. I'll handle this shit myself. If you want something done right, you have to do it yourself anyway. I get in my car and pull out into traffic. Now I'm going to have to let this calm down and hit that bitch with the sonogram picture. I'll show her I can give Shane what she can't, and that will surely drive her over the edge.

TWELVE

This is it. Today, I finally get my life back. My forever with Shane will officially start now. After today, Harper will be gone and Emmie will be utterly useless once I'm done with them.

Sean should have already grabbed Gabriella and Mia. Honestly, I can't believe Gabriella survived taking two gunshots in the chest. She's recovered like nothing happened to her at all. This only makes me want to end her more.

Now for me to get Harper.

I watch Harper get up from the table she is sitting at, hug Emmie and Dallas, then make her way toward the restrooms. The glow she is displaying today at her baby shower is making me nauseous. She is so dramatic that she had to be put on bed rest. I know it's so she could hold on to Shane's attention even more. She is such a manipulative bitch.

"I'll be right back. I need to use the ladies' room." I stand up from the table.

"Okay, darling."

I walk into the bathroom just as Harper turns from drying her hands. In all the times I have seen her at Rock America, I've never given her any indication of how I truly feel about her. It's been the performance of a lifetime, hiding how much I hate the manipulative cunt who is ruining my life every chance she gets. But that is all over now. I don't have to pretend anymore.

Thank fuck.

"How are you?" Harper asks, looking like she thinks we're friends. Really? Friends? This bitch has tried to take everything from me. I can't even stomach looking at her. "You've been quiet today."

I lift my lips in a half smile. "Oh, you know me. I just like to sit back and take everything in." I step farther into the bathroom and set my purse on the sink. I don't look at Harper as I move some items in my purse around to get the gun I have hidden. The same one I shot Gabriella with. The one I've been dreaming of using to kill this whore beside me. "Have you enjoyed your day?"

"It's been perfect. It's still hard to believe this is happening. I never thought this day would come. Having a baby was a dream for me for so long that I didn't even believe the doctor when he first told me I was pregnant."

I nod, still shifting things in my purse, waiting for the opportune time to point the gun at her and make her leave with me. "Yes. I didn't believe it when Sean first told me."

But that was when my world turned dark. It was when I realized Shane was slipping through my fingers. Nothing I had done up to this point was splitting them up. It took me a little bit to come up with this plan, but I have Harper in my possession, and now I'm going to end her. Then, finally, I will take back what is mine. Shane will be mine, and we will live our forever.

Everything I have done, and what I am about to do, is for Shane. I am rescuing him from these crazy women who have hindered his life. I will destroy Emmie, Harper, and Gabriella by the end of this day. *Just a little while longer, Shane.*

Wrapping my fingers around the butt of the gun, I turn and point it at her. More specifically, at her belly. That baby is trying to come between Shane and me just as much as her fucking mother is. It has to be destroyed just as Harper does.

"What are you doing?" she asks as she wraps her hands protectively around her stomach.

"I'm taking back what was mine to begin with," I state with calmness.

"Yours?" she whispers.

"Yes. Mine," I reply, smiling at her so sweetly. "Shane was mine first, Harper dear. Didn't he tell you?"

"No," she whispers. "No, he didn't tell me."

I want to be mad at Shane for not telling Harper about me, his first love. His only *true* love. But I just can't bring myself to at this moment. I need to get Harper out of here without anyone seeing us.

"I thought the pictures would be enough to convince you that I'd had him first. But you couldn't take the hint. Then, you didn't even pay attention to the ultrasound picture I sent. Did he even show you? Or did he feel too guilty once he found out you were pregnant?"

"Was there ever a baby?" she demands, anger flashing in her purple eyes.

I shrug because it really doesn't matter at this point. "There was, but I didn't know who the father was. I couldn't keep it in case it wasn't his."

I'm losing time. If I don't get us out of here soon,

someone is bound to try to stop me. No way is this plan going to be ruined like all the others have been before.

"Let's go," I snap, stepping forward, causing Harper to retreat until her back hits the door and it pushes outward.

We step out into the hallway, the gun still pointed at her protruding belly. I don't understand why any woman would want to put herself through all of that for a crying monster. I can hear everyone still having a good time. Harper opens her mouth like she is about to scream for help.

"Do it. See what happens," I dare.

She quickly snaps her mouth shut. I press the gun against her belly and guide her to the exit. Harper cowers back as I open the door and the rain hits her. "Keep moving," I bite out and push her forward.

Harper stumbles a few times, and when I stop suddenly, she falls against the car. It is pouring rain, and we are both drenched.

"Helena...p-please don't do this. Shane will never forgive you if something happens to me," she pleads.

"What Shane doesn't know won't hurt him." I laugh at her.

I pop open the trunk and push Harper forward. She stumbles and falls into the trunk with a frightened cry. I push her legs the rest of the way in and shut the trunk.

Walking around to the driver's side, I open the door and get inside. After shaking off some of the water, I start the car and drive out of the parking lot.

It takes a little over thirty minutes for me to get to the farmhouse. I call Sean on the way. He's already secured that bratty kid of Emmie's and the bitch who ruined everything. I will take out the whole lot of them to get Shane back so we can finally start our life together.

The life that should have been ours to begin with.

The farmhouse I'm using to destroy them belonged to Sean's aunt on his father's side. She passed away about a year ago, and it's been abandoned ever since. It's out in the middle of nowhere.

Once I arrive, I step out of the car and open the trunk to get Harper out. I hold the gun on her, but the rain is making it hard for me to see.

"Get out," I command.

Harper manages to get herself out of the trunk after struggling for a few moments with her huge stomach—the cow. I hold the gun on her the entire time, refusing to help her as she grunts and pants for breath.

"Walk to that barn." When she hesitates, I push the gun into her big belly—hard—to show her I'm not playing around. She quickly begins walking in the direction of the barn.

I push her into an old stall filled with dried-up hay. I had a new door with steel bars installed. The previous door wouldn't have held a child, it was so rotten. I slam the door shut, locking it, and walk out of the barn. Sean is waiting for me outside.

"Light it up," I demand of him.

He walks around the side of the barn where he has put the gasoline. The only person missing from inside this barn is Emmie. But her daughter will have to do. Emmie losing Mia will bring her a lifetime of agony. She'll be destroyed, I'll get Shane back, and then I'll add to her misery by kicking her out of Shane's life. The way I see it, she loses her child and she loses her brother, and I take what's mine and live happily ever after.

Sean begins pouring the gasoline around the outside of the barn. "Helena, the rain is going to cause us a problem here."

"It will stop eventually."

"The ground is still damp because of it," he argues.

"Drench the place, Sean. I don't care if it is a slow burn. That means they suffer longer."

When Sean finishes, we head to the farmhouse to wait for the barn to catch fire.

THIRTEEN

"This is taking forever," I complain.

"I tried to tell you that the rain made the barn damp, even on the inside. It's not going to ignite like you want it to. But it's trying. You can see the smoke from here."

"I want them dead," I whine. "Turn that stupid shit off." I can't stand the sound coming out of that small old-style television. The rain is causing it to be nothing but static. "Go make sure the barn is still burning. That fucking rain has messed up all my plans. I don't want it to stop burning before it gets to the good parts."

Sean stands and steps out of the room. "You're a twisted bitch, cousin."

"Who cares? I paid you well for helping me. Now go do as I said. It shouldn't take too long before the thing starts falling. When it does, call me so I can come watch."

Sean stomps his way through the house, and I began thinking about what Plan B would be if the damn thing doesn't go up in flames. I leave the kitchen and use the small bathroom in the hallway.

The rain has washed away my makeup, so now my

birthmark is exposed. As I stand there looking at my soaked reflection in the mirror, I hear a loud scraping sound coming from the living room area, along with footsteps.

Sean is done that quickly?

"Sean?" I call out. "Are you back already?"

I enter the room just as that bitch Gabriella is trying to exit out the back door.

"You!" I cry out in surprise and rage. Fuck, this bitch is nothing but trouble. I should have had Sean pop her earlier. "I've had enough of you."

"Same here, bitch." Gabriella turns and glares at me.

I reach around and pull the gun from the back of my waistband and point it directly at her face, grinning when she pales.

"Fuck," she whispers.

I've really had enough of this bitch getting in my way. If she would have just kept her nose out of my business to begin with, she would be safe with her rocker hottie right now. But no, she had to go and try to play hero, and now I have one more person to deal with before Shane and I can finally be together.

"I'm going to end you once and for all, Moreitti," I promise as I step toward her with my gun still pointed at her head.

"It's Bryant now, bitch." She turns and starts running.

After a pause, I take off after her. Several times, I have to regain my footing because the ground is wet. I see Gabriella with a phone to her ear.

"Damn it, she's going to ruin everything again," I whine.

Fuck, Sean should have thrown out her phone and not brought it here. They have probably been tracking it all along. *Fuck!* I take off running faster. I have to stop her.

Even with the distance I am from her, I can hear Shane

asking about Harper. He's fucking asking about Harper? No! He is supposed to love *me*. He does love me. My rage burns hotter than the flames now overtaking the barn in the distance. No way am I going to lose it all.

I stop running, point the gun at Gabriella, and pull the trigger. I watch with pleasure as she falls on her face, but she quickly jumps to her feet and takes off running into the surrounding woods.

For a brief moment, I begin to question myself and Shane. Did he ever love me? Is this all in my head?

I shake myself out of it.

No, Shane loves me. Emmie made him love that simpleton. Harper manipulated him into believing he loved her. He didn't *want* to love her. He loves me.

"He loves me. He loves me. He. Loves. Me," I chant over and over again.

I've got to catch Gabriella before Emmie and her gang of suits show up and rescue them all. I got sloppy this time. I didn't think about cell phones being tracked. I sure as hell didn't think this little bitch would get out of a locked stall in the rickety old barn.

I take off running after her. She can't get far; she's been shot in the leg, but I have no idea which direction she went.

Then I see him.

The rock hottie who is married to Gabriella.

Shit, they're here.

He doesn't see me sneaking up behind him, and then I hear her.

"Liam!" she screams, alerting him—and me—to her whereabouts. I change direction and run toward her, but so does Liam.

I get to her first. But he isn't far behind me, and he throws himself over her body to shield her.

"Don't do this," Liam pleads with me. "She's done nothing to you. Let her go and take me. I'll do whatever you want."

I can't help but think how sweet and pathetic it is at the same time that this hottie rocker is willing to give up his life for her. It's only going to get him killed right along with her.

"She's done nothing but get in my way. Over and over again. She refuses to die!" I blow out a frustrated sigh. "She had to save the little brat, and even though I shot her twice in the chest, she just *wouldn't* die. I can't let her go now. She knows who I am and will tell Shane."

Liam shakes his head at me. "She won't. Shane won't know. Just let her go. Please. You can shoot me, I don't care. Let me take her place," he continues to plead, his deep voice cracking with emotion.

"Sorry, rocker boy. I can't do that. You're Shane's friend, and he won't like it very much if he has to bury his friends." I sigh and crouch down over them. "Besides, I kind of like you."

"Touch him and I'll gut you," Gabriella snaps at me.

"Ballsy, aren't you?" I laugh. She's got grit. If she'd minded her own damn business, we could have even been friends. Having double dates together with our rockers. Hanging out every now and then and loving our men. But no, this bitch had to go and fuck everything up.

"I got bigger ones than you, cunt-face."

"I can actually believe that. Definitely bigger ones than Reginald, that's for sure." My face twists in disgust at the thought of him touching me. "My husband never really had enough balls to satisfy me. Too bad you have to die, Gabriella. I might have liked you in another life."

"I can do without friends like you, psycho," Gabriella spits out. "Shane is going to kill you when he finds

Harper. Just wait. I wish I could see your face when he ends you."

"Shut up, Brie," Liam pleads. "She's going to kill you."

"Nah," Gabriella assures him, which stuns me. "How is she going to do that when Emmie's about to beat her ass?"

What?

A gasp leaves me as I stand, looking around. I glance behind me and then to my right. Finally, I hear her charge at me. I hit the mud, my head bouncing off the ground and thudding so loudly, it makes my ears ring. The force of the fall causes the gun to slip out of my hand, and it slides across the damp grass.

Emmie's hand slams into my face, and I can taste blood from my now-split lip. I can't get out from under her. She's raging harder than I can ever remember doing myself. She continues an unrelenting assault on me. She punches me again, and I hear my nose break but don't immediately feel the pain of it. She punches my face over and over. I'm useless to stop her.

Emmie twists us so I'm beneath her, before grabbing my head and beginning to sling it like a yo-yo. I can feel my hair ripping out at the roots, but the adrenaline keeps me from feeling the agony. My scream isn't from the pain but my anger, and I start to fight back, scratching her arms and her face with my nails.

I become disoriented, but I know I need to get my hands on my gun. It's the only thing that can save my life. And I can finally end Emmie. After all the years of misery this stupid bitch has caused me, I finally get to put a bullet in her.

"Emmie!" Gabriella yells. She must have seen that I have the gun in my hand. I press the gun into Emmie's stomach.

But Emmie seems to grow even stronger, and we fight for the gun, both of us trying to keep a hold of it. Emmie rolls me, attempting to get control of the gun. She hits her head, but all the while, she's still holding the gun, her finger on the trigger.

This is it.

All I ever wanted was for Shane to love me. And now, the woman who got in our way is going to end my life.

For a flash of a moment, I feel remorse.

I'm sorry, Reginald, for all the pain I have caused you. You deserved someone who could love you far better than I ever did.

I'm sorry, Shane.

I love you.

With Shane filling my mind and heart, I hear Emmie's manic laugh, and my world goes dark.

EPILOGUE

REX

I stand there looking out the window of my office. It is finally over; I am a free man. Free man in the unmarried way. It definitely hasn't been an easy process. I had to run announcements in a lot of newspapers that went unanswered. I had to swear under oath that I had no idea of her whereabouts, and then I had to wait. And wait.

I really had no idea where Helena was. Technically not a lie. I had an idea of what happened to her, but not where she was. I married a psychopath. I was just a means to an end for her. She had set her sights on Shane Stevenson from Demon's Wings, and when she failed, she used me as her backup plan. I didn't know it at the time. I honestly thought we fell in love. On my end, I fell in love with her, but she didn't feel the same.

I had felt sick at Harper's baby shower, listening to every detail unfold. I really didn't know the woman I was married to. She had been tormenting Harper right under my nose. The days she would disappear, saying she just needed some alone time, she was destroying tour buses, stabbing animals, trying to kidnap a child, and shooting

Gabriella Moreitti, now Bryant. Then she came home like she'd had an uneventful weekend at the spa.

It was a couple days after the baby shower that Shane and Emmie came to see me at Rock America.

"Rex, we don't have to worry about you, right?" Emmie asked.

"I don't know anything, and I don't want to know anything, Emmie," I responded to her, unable to wrap my mind around the fact that this had happened to me. "I still can't believe she was the stalker tormenting Demon's Wings—"

"Well, believe it, Rex," Shane interrupted. "That bitch was deranged."

"I know. I guess the part I can't believe is that she did all of those things and I had no idea about any of it." I shrugged. "But you have nothing to worry about. The police think she is on the run with Sean."

"I'm sorry, Rex. You didn't deserve to be dragged into any of this," Emmie assured me with a pat on my back.

"I found my press badge from the night I was supposed to interview Nik and Jesse," I said as I pulled it out of the top drawer of my desk. "She must have swiped it from me the night we spent together. I'm going to presume she kept it on her when she snuck into the secure areas to destroy your bus." I looked to Shane.

"I need to know my wife is safe now." Shane stood up from the chair he was sitting in.

I stood too. "I adore Harper. She is a great editor and an asset to this magazine. I'm glad this nightmare is over for her and all of you."

"We're all on the same page, then," Emmie chimed in.

I reached out my hand to Shane, and he took it.

"My wife is on the run and hiding out. That's enough for me," I said, shaking Shane's hand.

Shane and Emmie turned and walked out of my office, and we agreed never to speak of this again.

And now, here I stand with my divorce papers in hand. Free to live my life. I can put my past with Helena behind me. I went through the grieving process. Grieving the loss of the love I felt for her, not the loss of her. I had to work through the feelings one by one. If I hadn't, the hate would have consumed me. These divorce papers are the final piece to put my life back together.

Even though I knew Helena was never coming back, a part of me felt like I was cheating on her when I met Velinda Tilley, who had been hired to manage the HR department, and I experienced an immediate attraction. Velinda was the complete opposite of Helena in both looks and attitude.

The more time we spend together, the more attracted I become. At first, we would have lunch together, getting to know each other as friends. Then we started flirting. Now, I am free to take her out on a real date, and tonight is the night I'm making that happen.

I turn around and walk to my desk, placing my divorce papers in my bottom drawer. Then I grab my phone and send Velinda a text.

Me: Do you have lunch plans today?

I stare at the phone, waiting for her reply. Sometimes she replies right away, and other times it takes a little while. I feel like a teenager again, waiting for my crush to write me back. I'm excited to see where this relationship can go. If I'm honest with myself, I checked out of my marriage long before I found out what was actually going on.

I don't want Velinda to be a rebound; that's why I stayed true to my vows and didn't cross any lines. I needed all of my baggage packed up tight before I moved forward. That's the only scenario I felt was fair to me and to Velinda. We've discussed Helena, and she knows exactly what the rest of the world knows. Helena stalked Shane and his family and then went on the run and is hiding out, missing, whichever.

I'm deep in thought when I hear a tap on my office door, bringing me back to the present.

"Come in."

The door opens and in walks Velinda. She looks beautiful in her gray pencil skirt and lavender top. Her strawberry-blond hair is pulled back in a low bun with a few ringlets curling around her face.

"Hey there," I say, moving around my desk to meet her as she walks into my office, shutting the door behind her.

"I was on this floor when I got your text, so I figured I would come see you."

"I'm glad you did," I murmur, walking closer to her.

"I don't have lunch plans." She smiles at me. Her smile is gorgeous, and her blue eyes sparkle

"You do now," I respond. "And if you're not busy tonight, you have dinner plans too."

"It's final!" she exclaims and throws her arms around my neck. I wrap my arms around her waist and hold her close to me. She smells exquisite. She's told me before she uses an Egyptian oil instead of any type of perfume. Her scent is driving me mad and making my dick swell with excitement. I want to eat her up, tasting every inch of her skin.

"Yes, it's final. I'm a free man."

For now, I think to myself.

· · ·

TWO YEARS **later**

"I can't. I can't do this!" Velinda screams as she crushes my hand in hers.

"Precious, you can do this. You can do anything you put your mind to," I soothe.

"Okay, Mrs. Brannen, one more big push and your little girl will be here, and you can rest," Dr. Moyer tells us.

Velinda bears down, still holding my hand with great strength. The next sound I hear is our daughter's cries filling the room.

"You did it, my precious. You did it." I plant kisses on her forehead, tears streaming down both of our faces.

"Would you like to cut the cord, Mr. Brannen?"

I take the surgical scissors that are being handed to me and cut where I'm directed to. The nurse in the room takes our little girl over to get her cleaned up.

"I love you, Velinda. Thank you for giving me this amazing gift."

"I love you, Rex."

That night, I sit in the recliner chair in the private hospital room and hold my daughter in my arms as her mommy gets some sleep. My perfect family.

I don't think about the past anymore. I have more than I ever thought I would with my precious Velinda and our sweet Melissa.

PLAYLIST

"Unsaid" by Angels Fall
"The Scientist" by Coldplay
"Skinny Love" by Birdy
"Every Little Thing" by Carly Pearce
"Hearing Damage" by Thom Yorke
"I'm Gonna Show You Crazy" by Bebe Rexha
"Gasoline" by Halsey
"Different for Girls" by Dierks Bentley ft. Elle King
"Always Remember Us This Way" by Lady Gaga
"A Drop in the Ocean" by Ron Pope
"Someone You Loved" by Lewis Capaldi
"Back to Black" by Amy Winehouse
"Wrong Side of Heaven" by Five Finger Death Punch
"Bring Me to Life" by Evanescence
"Monster You Made" by Pop Evil
"Give You Up" by Dido
"Wrecking Ball" by Miley Cyrus

FINAL NOTE FROM LONNIE AND TERRI ANNE

Some of you may be asking yourself why we created a story for Helena.

The answer is quite simple, we needed content for Helena to bring her to life on your TV screens...along with all of the beloved characters of The Rockers...Series.

SURPRISE!!!

Get ready for Emmie, Nik, Jesse, Layla, Drake, Lana, Shane, Harper, and all of your other favorite characters from The Rocker... Series Universe. We are very excited to let you know that The Rockers... TV series is currently in development.